slighted.

slighted.

Chad V. Broughman

Etchings Press
Indianapolis, Indiana

This publication is made possible by funding provided by the Shaheen College of Arts and Sciences and the Department of English at the University of Indianapolis. Special thanks to the students who judged, edited, designed, and published this chapbook: Abigail Bailey, Olivia Cameron, Desteni Guidry, and Liza Harris.

UNIVERSITY *of* INDIANAPOLIS

Published by Etchings Press
1400 E. Hanna Ave.
Indianapolis, Indiana 46227
All rights reserved

etchings.uindy.edu
www.uindy.edu/cas/english

Printed by IngramSpark

Published in the United States of America

26 25 24 23 22   1 2 3 4 5

ISBN 978-1-955521-06-2

Cover image by
Joel Kramer
Cover design by
Abigail Bailey
Interior design by
Desteni Guidry

~ Table of Contents ~

For my beloved Erin...

~teeth~

Basil stuffed the pliers deep into his mouth, tried clasping them down on the backmost molars, but the handles were wide for his jaw, stretching and thinning his lips. He paused, looked out of the barn loft. Hundreds of winking stars dotted the sky. The expanse made him feel less alone, connected him to the other deserters, hiding in thickets or cellars or icehouses, pondering ways to mutilate themselves, all of them desperate to sidestep Mr. Lincoln's God-forsaken war.

When the vice gripped, he clamped down fast. A low click. Bone on metal. But he couldn't pull, just held steady, everything tight as saddle-stitch. He counted to three in his head, pushed against the wood planks and dug his feet into the floor. His eyes darted back and forth, drinking in every detail of the stage he was on. The one he'd still be on after prying out his teeth—an even bigger yellow-belly than he'd thought possible.

Then his mind slipped back to boyhood, the day his softness was made clear. He had walked into the barn as a heifer was being prepped for butcher. Grandpa was hooking the steel gambrel into the tendons of its hind legs while Pa cranked the winch, the hulking carcass raising up like a great spirit. The veins along its neck had been opened and blood soaked the straw beneath, staining it a rich purple. He stared at the thick, matted coat, the hemorrhaging frame, its severed head atop a hay bale—sitting upright, normal as could be, as if cows were made that way—then he met the dead eyes. Big and blank and wet. His heart thrashed against his eight-year old chest and he dizzied, emptying his stomach on the ground. Pa stared him down, shook his head, making several tsk sounds with his tongue before turning away.

That same floating feeling was upon him now, teetering on a tightrope, nothing but air. And a rusty pair of pliers in his fist. "Enough," he said aloud, then filled his lungs, squeezed the handles, knuckles white, sweat cold on his forehead. Everything stilled. *Now. Do it now, you daisy.* He cursed the day he was born and wept for his wife, his dead pretty Stella that he couldn't save after she slipped under the ice. Couldn't bring himself to go in after her. His brain screamed—jump in, try something, anything—but the ice cracked all around and his feet stayed planted. He stood motionless, calling out her name, his heart hardening to a slab, forever lodged between his soul and someplace else. The gutlessness rang louder than his sobs as he baby-stepped back to shore, fishing creel in tow.

He speaks to Stella now, tells her that he can no longer bear to smile. You said you loved my grin, that it gave great light. So when I think of how I failed you, in every way a groom can fail his bride, there's no other choice. Thought about putting a pitchfork through my manhood like the fella over in Marquette or chopping off my trigger finger, but prying out my teeth feels right, plundering anything good you fancied in me, like my hogwash smile. When I'm done with my chewing teeth, I'll wrench out the front ones, too.

Basil let the pliers slip from his hand, watched them hit the hay, open like legs. He called himself a milksop, leaned back against the nearest post and tapped his head against it, lightly at first, then harder with each hit. He begged God to strike him down, punish his cowardice. "Lord. I beg you!" Quickly, the pleading turned to fury and threats. "What would it take?" he asked. "Break more commandments? Is that it?" He was whirring too fast to remember all of them, so he spat them as they came to mind. "I'm gonna put other Gods before you," he said. "I swear it. And I won't keep the Sabbath no more, either. So smite me, Lord! Please! I'll start stealing, too. Then I'll use your name in vain!" He sucked in through his nose, then exhaled, "Damn You! Damn You to Hell!"

...

Basil woke to the hiss of a barn owl perched nearby. It turned its ring-shaped head toward him, glassy black eyes, judgment on its stolid face. The space was drenched in the faint blue of dawn. He grabbed his jaw with a thumb and fore-finger, thinking maybe he'd gone through with it.

A wave of relief tried rolling through, but shame quickly dammed it. He picked up the pliers again, turned them over in his hand, reared them up, chin height. His heart pounded in his mouth as he guessed at the pain, the aftermath. *Will my face ache forever? Push and pull like the tide? What does a pile of teeth look like? Broken molars gathered like tiny white stones. Will my words wobble?* Then he calls to mind the county commissioner tacking the manifesto to the front of town hall— "Notice of Drafting!"—and he riding past, blocking it from his mind. But now, come morning, conscription will knock at his door.

Basil rolled over, looked up at the ceiling and counted the rafters, twelve in all, remembering how he hauled them up himself, one by one. And how that night, Stella rubbed her soft palms against his spine until the twinge subsided. He hungered for that moment, yearned to live an eternity with her hands on his body, smoothing out the pain. No diffidence. No filthy war. Still hopeful for children. All his false fronts still intact.

As he moved the pliers toward his face a final time, his chest thumped again, beating his ribs till he thought they might crack. He inhaled through his nose, eyed the tool shaking in his fingers as if someone else was holding it. He opened his mouth wide, slammed his eyes shut—then idled there, trembling forever on the edge of fight or flight—

~check mate~

"'Ain't right. Men don't think about shit like that."
Dad's voice was big, and the house's insulation scant.

On the other side of the wall, Michael leaned in, listening for Ma's reply.

"I know, dear, it's a strange thing. But he's still our boy." Through the meager paneling, Michael felt Ma's strain, trying to placate her husband and protect her frail son.

"Nah. If a boy of mine was feeling bad about himself, he'd run around the block a time or two, lay off the beers. He wouldn't stick his fingers down his fuckin' throat."

"He'll hear you." Ma's voice shifted downward. "It's Christmas, let's not do this."

In the stillness that followed, Michael continued wrapping presents with his little sister, Vanessa, as they waited for their parents to emerge. Coming home was a mistake. He hadn't visited since last winter and was down another six pounds, back under one-twenty. At 5' 11", he knew how wilted he was, but thinking about it never changed anything. Besides, he'd already set his new goal: 115.

After he'd fainted at the student union, the counselor at the campus clinic told him to take time off. A master's degree can wait, she said, you're not well. She wrote down a couple of numbers on a sticky note and handed him an arm full of pamphlets. Because Michael thought she was nice, he waited until he got to his apartment to throw them away.

In the trash can, on top of the pile, a flyer with a scrag-gy woman standing in front of a mirror, no makeup, mouth agape, stared up at him. Her right hand was balled up, the knuckle of her index finger wiping away a shiny tear. Her left, palm up, held a clump of hair, the strands hanging down between slender fingers.

When hair fell out, that's when he'd surrender.

A week later, he had to follow through on his prom-ise. For several minutes, he stared at the patch of scalp, blank and pale, reflecting in the mirror, too nervous to acknowl-edge the coarse, black proof that tangled in the tines of his brush. The coming symptoms frightened him, but going home, into the awkward arms of his broken family, scared him more.

Call on your family, the doctor had said, they might surprise you. At that moment, he had let himself hope. May-be, just maybe, he thought. But then, he walked through the front door.

Ma brought her hands to her face, the horror showing in her wide, glistening eyes. "You look so handsome." The clumsy fidgeting of her hands exposed growing embarrass-ment.

Over her shoulder, Michael caught Dad's eyes. They gave each other a slow nod, then he retreated back into Ma's embrace and Dad back into his newspaper.

Pressing a strip of glossy ribbon between his thumb and the scissor blade, Michael pulled the blade toward his bony chest.

"Ta-da! A curlicue. Looks like one of those Cinnabons," he said, cocking his head, examining his work, "Without all that sticky stuff."

Though he smiled, his thoughts were about how feeble he must look and sound to Vanessa, she, a high-schooler, and he, a twenty-four-year-old skeleton with a thin voice and loose teeth.

"My wrapping is terrible," she said. "Looks like a papier-mâché project."

Michael looked at the slipshod mess in her lap and chuckled.

"Yeah, by a preschooler maybe," he said, then poked her with his elbow till she laughed.

In front of them, just above the television, was a long shelf supported on each end by a thick corbel, the classic kind with loops and tendril-like carvings. Dad had stained the wood a hard brown, almost burgundy. To Michael's recollection, it had always held the same knick-knacks: Ma's fairy figurines, a couple of vases filled with glass flowers and smooth, polished rocks, a framed Ansel Adams with a wide, gray river winding behind a jagged, snow-capped mountain, and in the center of it all, were the trophies.

For Vanessa, there were several, all from 4-H, the

old-fashioned kind with wide-handled chalices. Even though the gold coating had begun to peel, Ma kept them showcased. For Michael, there was just one, but it was tall and held its sheen. Regional Champion. A white-yellow plaited wrestler stood poised for a take-down, arms open, waist height. On the wood base, etched into a small square plate, was a passage: Believe in yourself, when no one else will. The letters were tiny, you had to step in close to read them.

From time to time, though less vividly now, Michael envisioned Coach hunkered down on the mat, eye level with a wrestler about to be pinned. He'd speak those words as if the boy wasn't twisted up like a pretzel, mounted by a competitor, with dozens watching from the stands. Coach could always make it seem like only the two of you were in the gym. Even when Michael wasn't the one being driven from the throes of defeat, he relished in those moments. The hope felt good, as did knowing that he was part of something bigger than himself, a necessary spoke in the wheel of a team.

That was a world ago, back when the only reason for shedding pounds was to make the lower weight class. For hours, Michael would spit into his red solo cup (the one he held between his knees so the teachers couldn't see it) just to lose an extra ounce or two. He ate only oranges, day after day. And sometimes, when the laxatives took hold in class, he'd have to sprint to the bathroom with his head flimsy and light, tottering like a paper airplane. It all mattered back then; there was a purpose to it.

Michael didn't blame Coach. He knew the man's heart was good. Push the sissy kid into a sport, he probably thought, give him a place to fit in. Hell, it worked, for awhile. Through his junior year, Michael was a varsity wrestler and a damn good one. Folks stopped calling him a pussy, even Dad.

Then Michael kept molting, long after the seasons ended.

...

The bedroom door made a low whoosh sound against the nappy carpet when Dad pulled it open and headed to the living room, the floor groaning under his heavy steps. When he first came into view, he slowed to a stop, eyes narrowed, lips tapered out. Michael hoped it was a sign of compassion, maybe Dad realized that the house was too small for all his hateful words. But he passed them by, wordlessly, and plunked down in his recliner in the far corner. Per usual, Dad fanned out the *Michigan Daily* with great effort, covering his bristly face.

"Did you see Michael's wrapping," Vanessa called to him. "Looks better than when Macy's does it, don't you think?"

Dad bent the newspaper and peered over it. "All looks the same to me, fancy paper and bows," he said, then shook his head in a broad, sluggish sweep and righted his *Michigan Daily.*

Before Vanessa could respond, Michael pushed his finger to her lips, stricken by how spindly it looked next to her fresh, pink cheeks.

Dad turned the page, rustling the paper like it was fighting him, then resumed reading. Though his thick fingers covered some of the lines, Michael could see the date—December 23, 1981—and a headline: *Adam Walsh's Story: Gone Too Soon.* Beneath the caption was the famous picture of the young boy, the one on all the "Missing" flyers—red baseball cap with a white, cursive C, holding his little league bat, mussed hair in his eyes. He recalled the day Adam's severed head was found.

By college, Michael had learned to hide his emotions, or at least curb them. He did that day, too, recalling the words of his history teacher after tearing up during a documentary on the Holocaust. Stop wearing your heart on your sleeve, Michael, you're too soft. But thinking of Adam's terror when the stranger first manhandled him proved too much. He wondered if the little boy called out for his mother, his father, or if he stayed silent, afraid to cry.

Dad folded the paper down to a single column, burying the article. It held no interest to him, Michael presumed. A curl of wooly black hair fell over Dad's high forehead, and it bothered Michael that he did not brush it away.

In Vanessa's slanted brow, Michael sensed her urge to petition Dad again. He mouthed "no" and from inside the bag next to him, pulled out another gift to be wrapped. It was Dad's. A custom built box for chess pieces, made of dense, richly beige rosewood, finely textured with a sleek finish.

Michael turned his back so Dad could not see the gift, the one he'd saved for most of the year and sent back twice. First the hue wasn't right, too dull; the second time there was a small mar on the lid. He picked up a tube of silver paper with a pattern of tiny bells and dark green holly and looked to Vanessa. She nodded in approval.

"Dinner's ready," Ma beckoned, stepping into the living room.

She smoothed her bulky apron with both hands, her eyes roving from Vanessa to Michael, eventually fixing on Dad. Her anxiousness was weighty, and Michael hurt to know his presence was the cause. He wanted to grab her chafed hands and hold them in his own, but that wasn't how they did things.

"Damn left-wings," Dad grunted. He flicked the newspaper with the back of his fingers. "Now this Chavez duck is whining 'bout more rights? And I'll be damned if all these bleeding hearts ain't doting on him like he's some kinda hero. These God-forsaken liberals are plowing this country under. I tell you what—"

"Can you put that down, honey?" Ma asked. "Come to the table."

"I'm eating in here." Dad snapped the paper again.

From the floor, Michael thought his father looked smaller, especially perched behind all the world's affairs. He pictured himself marching over to Dad's chair, crouching down till they were nose-to-nose. In an even keel, he would say, "You're a mean son of a bitch. Stupid, too."

Michael thought about all the strings attached to Dad's love. How when you're weak, he walks away, but when you're steady, he takes you fishing.

In middle school, when the boys started blowing kisses and calling Michael a faggot, Dad had said, stop acting like one. The worse the jeering, the quieter Dad became, eventually passing Michael by on his way out the door alone, pole in hand. It was only later, after Coach recruited Michael for wrestling, that Dad came back around.

At tournaments, he could be heard above the crowd, shouting things like, "That's my boy," and to whoever would listen, he would tell stories of how they used to tangle together on the floor, beaming with pride at the son he helped to shape. Yet after the last match, when the weight kept coming off and the nosebleeds started, Dad began his final retreat.

Then the bullying reignited, more creative, more intense than ever. Things bottomed out when Principal Miller showed up on their doorstep for a home visit to tell Ma and Dad about the boys who held their son down in the shower and pissed on him, one-by-one.

Michael spied from the hallway, listening intently, trying not to see Dad's deadpan expression. It hurt more than the stiff urine still caked in his hair. Miss Miller told them that the boys called him an easy target because—then she inhaled through her nose and pulled back her shoulders—he acts like a girl and never fights back. At this, Dad held up his hand and said he had heard enough while Michael crept to his room unseen.

Through his bedroom window came the familiar clank and clatter of Dad rummaging for his fishing gear, followed by the crunch of his truck tires against the pea stone as he left for the river.

...

Michael sat the gift-wrap on the floor then pushed the chess set across the carpet, stopping it at Dad's feet. He hadn't thought his actions through, he just wanted to keep the peace. So when Dad asked what the hell he was doing, Michael fumbled.

"I taught myself to play," he finally said. Dad didn't smile, but he didn't turn away either. "I remember, no matter who came by, you always asked if they knew how to play. No one ever did."

Dad picked up two of the knights and was rolling his thumb across them, tenderly, like stroking a rabbit's foot. A wordless void ensued, but Michael fought his instinct to fill it, waiting out the silence.

"I'll get my board," Dad said. Then, before heading toward the hall, he added, "Those pieces. You know, the ones you bought there. They're good ones."

They played well into the night. Only a handful of words were exchanged, mostly mutterings from Dad, and an occasional "damn" from both of them.

Michael had read through the "how to" guide that came with the chess set, garnering a loose understanding of castling a rook. For the first couple of games, Michael kept his king and both rooks in place, peeking at Dad now and again, basking in his furrowed forehead. When the time came, he slid the stately king to the right, slow and dramatic, then set the rook queenside and brushed his hands together. Dad made a low sigh, followed by several clicks of his tongue.

The mood was dense, but there was favor in it. Michael saw the quick glances between Ma and Vanessa as they made up reasons to keep walking by. He was gladdened by their tiny smirks. For a fleeting moment, he swore he could feel Dad's blood pushing through his own veins.

Though he lost every game, Michael made Dad work for the wins. Then, at the end of the last match, as he feared it would, fatigue set in. For him, it wasn't just feeling tired or weary, he could fight that. It was wading through a muddy swamp wearing concrete shoes, bearing boulders on his back. It was jet-lag and a hangover at the same time. It was full-tilt, every time, and always, always crippling.

When Dad began to arrange the pieces for another game, Michael had to confess his feebleness.

"I'm tired," he said. But his father continued to assemble the game, positioning the pieces just so.

"I can't play anymore."

"Nonsense, boy. You can, too."

"Look at me, Dad."

With bishop in hand, Dad stopped and raised his head. Michael watched his face slacken as his mouth shrank into a straight line. Dad leaned back and lowered his gaze to the board. Michael said good night, knowing that a slight nod was the most he could hope for.

...

It wasn't until late afternoon that Michael made his way to the kitchen. Standing at the sink, arms up to her elbows in cloudy suds, Ma dipped her head at him, offering half a grin. The Christmas Eve spread was already on the table, mirroring the Last Supper, a blend of spices amidst the shaky optimism. Outside, a corn-yellow sun shone down upon the blinding white snow.

The three of them sat at the family table, breathing in the newly baked bread, the sweet, buttery smell of pumpkin pie, and the heady aroma of roasted turkey. They pretended Dad wasn't a couple arm's lengths away, choosing to sit in the other room as usual.

"Smells good, Ma. Can't wait for the—" Michael's front tooth loosened. He pinched it with his fingers and jiggled it some, then spat it into his hand. The familiar sour of his stomach had leaked into his mouth. He no longer had to retch for the fire to begin, just the thought of food caused the briny taste to creep up his throat and coat his yellow teeth.

"Was that your tooth?" Vanessa blurted.

"Well," Ma cut in, her neck clenched, "the relish might be a bit tart."

She handed her son a tissue, discreetly, and patted Vanessa's head, just once. Michael blotted at the hole in his mouth. "I used apple cider vinegar this year," Ma said, before turning back toward the counter where she braced herself against the laminate.

Michael watched her shoulders rise and fall. He thought her magnificent. His gutlessness felt big, conspicuous. Year after year, as she pacified Pa's pride at the expense of her own, he'd never risen up, never tried to protect her.

Like the winter Dad crashed his Ford Thunderbird into a grove of hardwoods but told the neighbors Ma did it. Vanessa was only seven. At dinner that Sunday, she asked Dad why he told everyone at church that Ma wrecked the car.

"That's grown-up business, Vanessa," Ma said.

"But you can't even drive. How—"

"Pass the sweet corn, dear." Though Vanessa quieted, she kept her face wrenched in defiance of the mistruth. Michael merely stared at his mashed potatoes.

Or the time Dad applied for a supervisor job at the foundry, and Ma slaved over his inquiry letter. After Dad got the promotion, the new boss came for dinner.

The man, with a round, doughy face and a bulging paunch that stretched the green diamonds in his argyle sweater, handed Ma a bottle of Merlot and said, "Congratulations ma'am. You must be proud." Then he shook off his coat, saying, "And that letter. Your husband is a poet."

Dad put his arm around Ma's shoulder, heavily, and snatched the bottle with his free hand.

"I sure married me a looker," he said. "Didn't I?" As Dad studied the label, head down, he continued, "Yeah. She ain't too bright, but she's a pretty gal."

Ma fidgeted then drew in her breath, stood tall and nodded at both men fully. Though his lungs squeezed and his heart pounded loud and clumsy, Michael stayed silent. As Ma ushered everyone toward the dining room, she winked at him, her eyes wet and glowing, as if to say, take note son, here's what strength looks like.

…

Michael reached for another tissue and dabbed at his mouth. Vanessa began humming "Little Drummer Boy," and he joined in. Observing his mother from behind, he marked how her once solid frame had begun to bend under the burdens of age and worry.

I'm sorry for never saying sorry.

"How about more turkey?" Dad barked from his chair. Michael turned to Vanessa and parodied him, crossing his eyes, exaggerating a frown. She giggled. So did Ma. Having diverted their attention, he tried to sustain it. He lifted a heaping spoonful of relish to his chin.

Let them see me eating, give them some short-lived cheer.

He paused. *Do it!* he berated himself. *This isn't about you right now.* With great flair, he thrust the moss-green mound into his mouth. The peppery dill mingled with the salty remnants of blood. Vanessa squirmed in her chair while Ma managed a thin smile. Feeling bolstered, Michael fought the gag reflex.

Knowing the new cavity would cause a lisp, Michael could only smirk in response, close-lipped. If his 's' sounds became more sibilant now, they'd be deafening. The thought of sputtering made his heart flutter, then skip, and there was still dinner to get through. Michael tamed his breathing—

In through the nose, out through the mouth, just get to the bathroom.

He began filtering sentences through his mind till he found one without any tricky 's' sounds. Finally, he said carefully, enunciating each word, "I'm–heading–to–the–john," then heaved himself up from the table.

"Oh Michael," Ma begged, "You're not—"

"Let–it–go–Ma." The tiny blots of blood on his shirt were a rich, deep red, and he worried they would draw more attention, so he sidled into the hall like a crab, stopping at each family picture on the wall. Some of them, he'd celebrated; most he'd grieved. Though he knew the waiting would be brutal for Ma and Vanessa, he paused longest before the bathroom door, studying a perfectly hung picture of his parents in their younger years. Ma wore her Sunday best, a lavender taffeta dress and matching bell-shaped hat, and Dad was in his dress blues, vivid and crisp, his ample, dark hair coiffed just right. Before stepping into the bathroom, Michael turned back to Vanessa and through the hole in his front teeth, wriggled his tongue at her. This time, she did not laugh.

Michael had learned to muffle the retching by turning on the faucet and the fan, or by flushing the commode. He'd tell himself to breathe through the twisting, quick breaths, followed by slow and constant ones. Sometimes, though, if the force was too much, his lanky frame would pull in all different directions, and he'd gasp or heave. Like now. Michael knew his family had heard it, but someone had turned up the radio, most likely Ma. Relief swept over him like a light wind. Her compassion made him want to resist the final purge, but experience had taught him not to waste energy on such futile things.

"Now light that yule log and grab your lover. It's the artist heard by more than any other on earth." The disc jockey's holiday cheer seeped through the vent, rude and bumbling in the stillness. Then, Bing Crosby's low tenor poured forth, "I'm dreaming, of a white Christmas..." and Michael tried to vomit again. Only bile. He could feel Ma's eyes on the door. Someone turned up the volume even louder.

"Turn that shit down!" Dad bellowed. After the music clicked off, Pa's ungainly movements banged through the kitchen and beyond. His voice resonated when he asked, "How long's he been in there?"

Michael felt the lull that followed, only the ting of a fork against a plate and the low drone of the furnace. In his mind, he saw Ma chewing desperately, pointing to her mouth and raising her shoulders in feigned ignorance while Vanessa looked out the window in insolence. More dead air. Michael's heart quickened, waiting for a slam or shout. When Dad asked 'how long' again, his pitch was cool, the words drawn out. He exhaled, not realizing he'd been holding his breath.

The doorknob rattled.

"Leave him alone," Vanessa said. Her voice was sharp, even lordly. Michael braced himself against the bowl, knowing Dad would burst through it before he could pull himself up. One more jolt of the knob was all it took.

The disillusionment of the scene shown in Dad's countenance; his only son kneeling by the toilet, the stench of rancid puke. And the shame. Dad's eyes swelled, his jaw set.

"Get up, boy." He bent over Michael and grabbed his arm, but paused. They both looked at Dad's fist, wrapped around Michael's meager arm like a gear shaft. Dad held tight for a moment longer then loosened his grip.

"I'm afraid, Dad."

"Of what, for shit sake? Some meat on your bones?"

"No. That's not—"

"Then what? Food? Is that it?"

Michael shook his head, slow at first, but Dad persisted. As the pitch in his voice heightened, so did Michael's sway.

"Afraid of food? Then eat, damn it. I don't get—"

"Of you." The room closed in. Michael felt a hard drain as if he'd crested the top of a rollercoaster, stomach floating. "Isn't that what you want, Dad? To be feared?"

Dad cast down his eyes. Turning on his heel, he left without another word. Only a slight footprint in his wake, as well as a few spatters of pink toilet water and a thread or two of hair.

Michael laid his spent body on the cold, damp tile, listening for the rumble of Dad's truck, and his mind drifted to a future he might not see. To a fall afternoon, brisk and blue. To his parent's house, still and quiet. Without provocation, Dad would wrinkle up his paper and toss it aside. He'd turn toward the center shelf and stare at the little brass wrestler before rising from his Lazy Boy and stepping lightly to the couch where Ma sits. Silently, he'd stoop down before her and rest his head on her lap. "Tell me about my son," he'd say. The intimacy would startle her, and she'd look at the ceiling, balling up her fists. But just as quickly, Ma would fan out her fingers and bring them down gently, stroking Dad's thin, white hair.

"Well, he knew you cared," she'd lie. "And he was beautiful."

Michael made his way to the window and looked into the side yard then lay back on the floor and pulled his knees into his chest. Amidst the woe and burn, he savored the hope that came with Dad's truck, still parked in the driveway.

~unfolded~

"Yes, sir." I scoot my chair forward, not closer, just forward, and the wooden legs cheep against the floor. Instead of at his hip, I'm sitting just beneath his shoulder. No farther though, I tell myself, keep some distance, from his face, his gaze, his indifference. Against the sterile white sheets, his skin looks gray. I try not to feel anything, no sadness, no anger, no love; yet I feel all three, welled up and perched in my throat. I stare at the worn wallpaper above his head—fat, vertical columns, gold then yellow, then gold. The hush feels clumsy. I think, this cannot be comforting to him? Can it? But if rigid, thick silence is all a dying man wants, well, who am I not to oblige?

"Son." The word sounds like he put it through a colander, low and strained. And difficult to bare. In response, I simply tighten my cheeks and forehead, and lean in, a little. He raises his bony fingers and spans them out. For me to hold, I presume. But I let them hover. So he drops his hand on the bed and says, "Talk to me."

I can feel my face slacken. And the blood rush begins, pulsing hard, then harder. Below his knobby knuckle sits a heart monitor, the light is a dull, sickly red. I hope that it starts spinning or flickering—whatever—just fill this big, white space. Say something, I command myself. Fuck, say anything. We speak, at the same time:

"I don't know what to— "

"How are the—" then wait for one another to continue, my chest feels light and my heart skittish, like when you're about to run a race, and the starter's gun is up. This is it. I'm going to tell him. I'm going to say, you hurt me, Dad. And by God, he's going to hear me.

"Please, boy, you go," he says, then exhales, heavy. His lips are stuck together in the corners. I look between my knees and study the tile a moment—it's old but polished, with random black specks, I think they look like ants. I suck in hard through my nostrils, let my mouth bunch to one side, a half smile, and lift my head. His stare is iced over now, and blank.

When I open my mouth, his eyes idle, then, slow as pouring oil, they close.

~tiny mirrors~

Our senior year, Bridgette Wheeler poked holes in Dean Foster's rubbers. She told her best friend, Nikki, how she had straightened out a paperclip then speared the butt end through every condom in the pack. She provided all the gritty details with zeal and a bent smile. How she crept into Dean's new Dodge Charger while he was at wrestling practice, pulled them out of the glove-box and just started stabbing. How when some of the "slippery stuff leaked out," she was afraid of getting any on his door handle, so she licked it off her fingers. How it tasted like hairspray and felt nasty on her tongue, the way Jell-O leaves a film after you swallow it. When Nikki asked her why she wanted to get pregnant so bad, Bridgette answered plainly: "Dean ain't leaving me behind. Just 'cause he rolls around on a mat with a bunch of other guys, doesn't mean he should get his college paid for. Besides, University of Wisconsin?" she said, more like a question, "that's too far away. And, its like, cold city there."

That's when I stopped eavesdropping, tried to refocus on my Calculus quiz. Got a B- on that damn thing, ran out of time.

...

To this day, whenever I turn on the car radio, I cringe for a split second, hoping that lean voice of Crystal Gayle's doesn't slip through the airwaves and start knifing at the old wound, making me bleed again from that place that scabbed over. The place where I buried the fact that Dean Foster's run-of-the-mill life was my fault—I kept a secret that wasn't mine to keep. The place that jolts me back to '77 and "Don't It Make My Brown Eyes Blue" is playing in the high school gym. Most of us boys standing against the wall, wishing we were one of the few who had the balls to ask for a slow dance instead of side-stepping to the bathroom, pretending we had to piss whenever the d.j. played a song with less than a four count rhythm. I remember all eyes being on Dean and Bridgette—him with his hand crammed in the back pocket of her form-fitting Vanderbilts, the other stroking her feathered hair, furled out like the ocean's tide. And their hips pressed together tight. Everyone jawing about whether they were doing it or not. Andrew Martin declared, "When they're sucking face in the hall, I can see her tongue"—eyes wide, nodding up and down like he'd just discovered uranium—"that's how you know Bridgette's getting the Manwich." Then, in a sing-songy voice, Chad chimes in with, "Two all beef patties on a sesame seed bun," and both of them nicker like ponies.

Not me, though. I twisted and squirmed, begging God for the courage to bust between the lovers and scream, "Dean, your swinging fox, she's trapping you! The rabbit's gonna live, man!" yet knowing in my heart of hearts that I wouldn't. I mean, this was about destroying dreams and raising babies. Holy shit kind of stuff. But I stood still, holding up the wall, watching the disco ball shimmering silver like a fish's underbelly, praying like hell that those hundreds of tiny mirrors weren't reflecting my own underbelly—soft, splattering its sickening, yolk-colored bullshit across the floor, up the walls, and all the way into my future.

...

Took me years to come to terms with the real reason that I didn't tell Dean that night. Or ever. Truth is, I didn't want him to leave either. Not because I'd miss him, we hadn't talked since middle school, back when jocks became jocks, and the rest of us hovered on the fringe like shrubbery. It wasn't a boy meets boy kind of thing either. Sure, I was mere hedging in the landscape of my school days, but I was certain about some things.

Quite simply, I was afraid that Dean Foster might do better than me. I'd always been smart, that was my knack. And someone like him getting to go to college out of state because he was a bit more agile than most, well, it just wasn't fair.

Guess it's true what they say, if certain things go unsaid for too long, your penance is to absorb the silence, let it soak into your bloodstream and invade your chromo-somes. Like addiction or blonde hair or oily skin, it be-comes part of your genetics. Then, you pass along the guilt and self-doubt to your own kids. And they to theirs.

So, every Christmas as I make my way home, I take a little detour. Just past the Beaumont the Beautiful sign off Route 2, the one that reads "Come see us again" on the backside in red, swirly letters, and I turn left, head down Perkins Street. Through friends of a friend, I learned that Dean lives by Smith's Slaughterhouse in a ramshack-le two-story place with big wood shingles and a droopy overhang above the square porch, a concrete block. He drives the same Dodge, but the tires are bald now and one of the side-mirrors dangles down. I heard Bridgette left him for the lead mechanic at the Nuts & Bolts auto-shop the year after graduation and moved out by the county line. And that Dean only sees his daughter on the weekends. Though I've never seen it real time, I can imagine Dean pushing his little girl on the swings at the Beaumont Ele-mentary playground, having blanket picnics with bologna slices and cubed cheese. And her—creamy skin and thick, wavy hair like her mother's—not yet knowing that she'll probably never leave Beaumont either, that she'll never ex-pect just a little bit more than the village of barely 2,000 people, unworthy of a yellow splotch on a Michigan road-map. A red dot with a circle around it, only because it's the county seat.

Yet I ache, thinking, oh Lord, when did my brown eyes turn so damn green....

~featherweight~

In fifth grade, I had to write an essay on a topic I felt strongly about. I wrote mine about hunting and called it, *Murderers Amongst Us*. In it, I declared the act of shooting an animal to be homicide, denounced hunters to be barbarians. My teacher gave me an 'A' and drew two red stars by my name. For a few days, Ma taped it to the front of the refrigerator but always took it down when she heard Pa pulling in. I asked her why, and she told me there was no use upsetting him.

"Why would it?"

"It's about man things," she said, folding the essay in her hands. "Trust me, I don't understand them either." I must have looked at her funny because she quickly revised her statement, "I mean, all that macho stuff. Kind of silly, don't you think?"

That week, someone's fingers were caught in the belt feeder where Pa worked and the mill closed early. Ma was in the garden. By the time she heard Pa's truck, it was too late to get to the refrigerator. It was quiet at the dinner table, except for intermittent food talk, like "Pass the mashed potatoes" or "More peas?" And the bare space where my essay had been was awkward and blaring, may as well have been a naked stranger standing there. The next day was Saturday, and Pa left without a word. A few hours later, he returned, sloppy drunk. He stepped from the truck and ambled to the porch where Ma and I stood. In one hand was my essay, rolled into a cylinder; in the other, dangling from his index finger, was a new pair of boxing gloves.

They were Everlast brand, light brown and vinyl. "Already shaped, don't gotta make a fist," he said, turning them back and forth like a game show host. "Just slide your fingers in and they curl up on their own." When he pushed the gloves toward me, Ma stepped to my side, pulled me close and stroked my hair, hard. She told me to thank him for the thoughtful gift. But my tongue wouldn't move. Now I understood what she was trying not to say just days before. Pa thought me a milksop.

"Take 'em boy, they ain't gonna bite." I held out my hands and Pa put them on me—the foam padding soft, rubbery—and drew the strings tight. Though the gloves felt clumsy, like winter boots strapped to my hands, in that moment, I was the reason for the atta-boy gleam in his eye. Then, Pa returned to the truck, pushed his upper body through the open passenger window and reappeared with another pair of gloves, bigger ones.

My heart flopped. My face flushed red, hot.

Pa stepped near but said nothing, just tapped his padded hands together and nodded toward the yard. I looked to Ma, but she turned away. I plodded after him into the front lawn. Then, he stopped, spun around, and started ducking and diving, drunkenness making him sway some. Though Pa's sparring was gangly, I was terrified.

"Dukes up, boy," he said, dancing half circles around me. I stood like a statue. "Guard yourself," he shouted, jabbing just past my ear with his right, crossing with his left. I raised the gloves in front of my face, palms in, but my legs wouldn't move. The louder he yelled, the more immobile I became.

"Put 'em up, damn it!"

"I can't. I just—"

Pa stopped hopping and slowly lowered his arms until they hung at his sides. An eternity passed while he stared at me. I tried to maintain his gaze as best I could. His eyebrows pulled down and together. His lips narrowed, nostrils flared. Quick as a copperhead strike, he threw a right hook. We were like two pistons, his glove smashed into mine, then my own fist struck the bridge of my nose. My neck snapped, and I stumbled backward. I remember the sound of his laughter, big and devilish. It felt like the whole world was watching. Though the sting from the blow didn't come right away, my cheeks were burning. I wanted to run but that seemed even more humiliating. After regaining balance, I pulled myself upright to face him and a nervous chuckle slipped out, more like a high-pitched cheep to my own ears.

Pa was silent again, his eyes wet and glassy. My breaths were short, like I'd swallowed a cork and it stuck.

I tried to tug at the collar of my shirt but with my gloved hands, I couldn't grip it. Then I crossed my arms, uncrossed them, and crossed them again. At that point, the bite from Pa's punch set in. The skin in my face tightened, and my nose had a pulse. When my lower lip began to tremble and the tears welled up, I pleaded with myself, *stop squirming,* then the tears spilled out anyway. I cast down my eyes and thought, *Oh God, I am a sissy.*

Though I didn't look up, I could hear Pa ripping off his gloves, the vinyl scrunching and creaking. They thudded at my feet when he threw them down and traipsed past me, an uneven gait. I glimpsed over my shoulder in time to see him ascend the porch stairs. The sun had risen, and its rich, yellow rays were full across his back. I thought he looked like a god, a fearful one. Without turning around, he said woodenly, "Put the gloves away," then the screen door banged against the door frame.

I knew then that one day I'd recover from Pa's disappointment in me, but when I looked to the kitchen window just in time to see Ma duck out of sight, I was down for the count. It would take a lifetime to pull myself up off the mat, to figure out which of the three of us shamed her most.

~from under the porch~

Whenever little Warren plays in the park, Jane watches from the kitchen window. Sometimes she cries as his blonde hair, mussed and light, blows this way and that. And as he gambols in the fort he made between the butterfly bushes and swing sets, she wonders if he'll hate her some day for keeping him too close.

...

Jane saw him when she was just ten years old. Thin frame and sad, dirty face. The sky was the color of cement and the air damp. Mushroom weather, she thought. Her father agreed but told her not to stray past the barn. "We're new here, Janey," he said, his greasy hand patting the ground for a wrench from under the family's light-green Hudson Hornet. Jane pushed it closer with her toe. "Not sure what's back there yet. It's off limits."

For a while, Jane searched the nearby groves, but not a single morel. Then she meandered to the tree-line, looked over her shoulder and veered into the forbidden stretch of woods. Once in the thicket, she walked faster, until the house and barn were out of sight. Her heart pounding at the disobedience. The ground was spongy from the winter melt, each step sinking down some. After clamoring over a lengthy knoll, a brown, grassless clearing emerged; in the middle, a slanted shack. There were big gaps between many of the two-by-fours. The makeshift chinking had crumbled. Only two windows—both on the second story—each holding twelve small panels, mostly cracked, with cardboard pieces covering the holes. At one time, the house had been painted, but the only proof was several dingy swaths of white near the gables. There was a fat rope tied around a metal pole and nailed to the far wall. A sheet was pinned to it, billowing and snapping in the cool breeze. Jane was afraid, but curiosity dwarfed her fear. She told herself the house must be abandoned and turned sideways so the sheets were out of sight, then crept like a crab toward the front.

Nearing the porch, Jane slowed, the suction noises lessening. A main floor joist was uneven, rising up to a stack of bricks used as a support pillar, then angling down again. Across the top, the wood planks were still in place but curled at the ends. Clumps of dormant grass filled the dark place between the porch and ground, except for one much trampled area.

The boy was in the shadows, chained to a corner post, a ramshackle collar around his neck. He peeked out. Pasty complexion. Wide, bulging eyes. An egg-shaped birth mark over his right brow, purplish-red, like an over ripe plum. Jane met his glance and held it. Beside him was an empty plate, remnants of stew were smeared across the ceramic.

A fork lay in the dirt and next to that, a tin cup. Jane felt light-headed, thought her knees might buckle. When she looked back to the boy, he was still fixed on her. Neither of them smiled, neither spoke.

Heavy footsteps thudded from inside. And their eyes darted toward the noise. The clack of work-boots grew louder. When the screen door squeaked open, Jane ran back into the grove, the rusty springs moaning as the door slapped against its frame.

...

Dinner was on the table. Her father asked her where she'd been but Jane could only shrug. The silence was mistaken for sass. For that, she was spanked. Though the belt stung, the little boy's dusty face stayed in the forefront of her mind, softening each blow. She never told anyone about the boy under the porch, knowing her father would only say—"that's a family matter, leave it be."

Months later, at the height of summer, Jane told her father that her belly hurt in order to skip church. She sneaked back to the rickety house with the rippling sheets and lopsided floor. It was the Assumption of Mary, so she figured a good two hours at least.

Several boards were nailed across the opening where the boy had been. The clothesline had been taken down, too. They were gone, Jane knew that. But she needed to look between the slats, convince herself that the boy had existed.

With her heart thwacking against her ribcage, Jane cupped her eyes and leaned in. She knew she was alone, but still, the fear of something jumping out made her shake. There was a heart-shaped indent in the dirt; inside it, the cup and soiled plate. She didn't know what she wanted to happen, so the wave of sadness came without warning. And she began to cry. Not a whimper, but an ugly, jerky sob. Jane wiped at her eyes then started pulling at the boards. So-so at first, but soon enough, she was straddling her legs, post to post, and wrenching each one free. The force from the final one cast her on her back and she lay in the moment of triumph before wriggling into the tiny hollow.

Jane leaned her head back, stared out at the vastness. She knew it wasn't the same, you can climb back out whenever you wish, she chided herself. But at least she could guess at his thoughts, his dreams, as he studied the same landscape day after day—far reaching meadows to the east and to the west, full firs and mighty hemlocks. Somewhere deep in her guts, Jane felt the boy's approval, swore he could feel her there. When the rain set in, she stuck her hands out, letting the mist gather on her fingers. She rubbed the cup and plate clean, hugged them against her chest and promised God, heart and soul, that one day, she'd love her own child fully, guard it like a soldier.

...

Warren looks across the street, and Jane ducks, waits. Then, she peeks through the window, making sure her boy is oblivious again, and pulls the frilly yellow curtains closed.

But not all the way....

~homecoming, and going~

In the skirmish between the strength of the lacquer and the passing of time, a clear winner had been declared at the Pure Heart of Mary Church. Though dulled, the nicks and dings more conspicuous, the pews were taller and straighter than Kyle remembered.

Ma lead him to the same place they had sat when Kyle was young and where she still did, apparently—left side, middle. As Kyle helped Ma pull off her coat, he made a sweeping scan of the same folks he remembered from his youth. They perched in their places, spaced apart like birds on a wire. He turned back around but could feel their eyes on him, a friendly welcome home to one of their own.

When he looked closer, Kyle saw grimness in their faces, in a way he never noticed growing up, a kind of lived-in look, marked by distinct, furrowed lines pulling their cheeks earthward. In their clear eyes, though, there was gentleness. Kyle did remember that, the soft miens of hardy worshippers. Year after year, these men and women endure Michigan's brutal winters: shoveling endlessly, wielding axes for bottomless supplies of firewood, and enduring icy winds that cut their faces. Though nature bowed their backs and flecked their skin, Kyle could never remember anyone complaining. Then, come spring, they expressed abundant gratitude for the reprieve of fresh rains, full-bodied smells of petrichor and bloom, accompanied by sweet, mellow bird songs.

Sitting in the nave again made Kyle anxious. A tree without bark, all its knots and scars laid bare for condemning. As if somehow, they had all heard the parting words of his fiancée just a few days before: "I don't feel excited when you walk in the room anymore," she said, then pecked him on the cheek, like a reward for a dog that fetched a stick. "We're good, Kyle, but I need great."

Deep down, he knew these people didn't know and even if they did, they would never judge him. This was his baggage, not theirs. It was only now that his demons had finally abated some, took a break from sucking his marrow dry. The more he thought about the vulnerable times of his adolescence, the more he remembered always ending up here, amidst this flock. The quiet kindnesses helped him sidestep any insecurities that should have arisen from growing up without Pa.

...

On Kyle's seventh birthday, they got word of an explosion at the iron ore mine over in Keweenaw County. Several colliers burned in its belly, but a couple managed to squirm through the wreckage, including Pa. But two days later, he died at the hospital, gas fumes had seared his lungs.

After that, the men of the parish always took Kyle on their father-and-son adventures—hunting and fishing. Some even made it seem like Kyle was doing them a favor by going. Even as a boy, Kyle knew what they were up to when they said things like, "Hold on to my pole a minute, will you, lad?" They would pretend to fiddle with their tackle boxes or fuss with their creels. Then—voila!—Kyle would reel in a hefty brown trout or occasional pike that they'd hooked for him.

Kyle knew none of them had needed his help, not for raising a barn, gutting a deer, or changing the oil. But he had wanted to learn such things, prove to them and himself that he could do anything if given the chance. One afternoon, after Kyle came home from felling a tree with Deacon Clyde and his two sons, he heard Ma in her room, thanking God for delivering such mentors to her son.

...

Sitting in that hard, uncomfortable pew, Kyle wondered how many of them had done it all because they thought he could never strike out on his own? Ironic, really. Flying away from the very source of courage that gave you wings.

The man who made it out of the Upper Peninsula, all the way to the City of Angels. Big time screenwriter. In the process, he had turned his back on the steadfast kinship that reared him, forgotten it could still exist. What had he really escaped? Their belief in one another? Their trust in something bigger than themselves?

Like a fierce Great Lakes tide, an unexpected sorrow swept over him. Kyle couldn't quite name it, but it was a thinner version of the void he felt at his Pa's funeral.

Though he had the urge to pray, Kyle decided it had been too long; it didn't feel right. Instead, he immersed himself in the soothing broth of wellbeing and safety. Nothing could hurt him here. Not in this hour. Not in this place.

His mind wandered, to the little landscaped sign just off Route 26, pride of the town: Beaumont the Beautiful. And the annual Lilac Festival each July, crowning the new Lilac Queen, grilling frankfurters, and binging on homemade pies made from the bounty of their backyards, rhubarb and boysenberry.

He thought, too, of all the loss and suffering the congregation had known. Yet they didn't seem to dwell in their hardships, never had. Not when the mine blasted open or even when a stranger came to town back in '81 and popped their bubble of immunity, bled out the lamb with one clean swipe of a blade.

...

The man had entered Miss Avery's classroom dressed

like a scarecrow, straight out of The Wizard of Oz. A tall, pointy hat with straw tucked underneath it, poking out enough to cover his ears. For a shirt, he wore a burlap bag that hung down to his thighs—big, plaid patches sewn on the sleeves. Under that were his knickers, patches on both knees. Kyle still remembers the rope that was cinched around his waist, dangling at his hip. He had nightmares about it for years after, what that man might have done with it in the quiet hours that followed.

And the painted nose, a perfect triangle, the color of dry dirt. Looked more like a blemish than a facial feature. His grin was lopsided, too.

Sometimes it replays in Kyle's mind in slow motion: the crash into reality that it wasn't a funny trick Miss Avery had planned—no game for the kids to figure out or play. The noiselessness as the stranger scoured the front row was excruciating, peering at all of them before settling on Lucille, then hefting her over his shoulder like a gunny-sack. Her eyes wide with terror.

Miss Avery furrowing her brow and cocking her head as she crept from behind her desk, slow as a spider. Her voice shaky and low but rising with every word: "Class? What is this? None of you know that man?"

Kyle had held his breath, letting it leak out gradually like a tire, praying the scarecrow man wouldn't hear him exhale or his heart thrashing and come back to take him, too.

Then Miss Avery's wail bounced off the lockers and ricocheted into the classroom. Some of the kids clapped their hands over their ears. One boy climbed under his desk and hummed, evenly, like an old space heater, as he rocked back and forth. Kyle hunched over, made himself as small as he could, and begged for Ma to come for him soon.

The town council closed the school for the rest of the week and forbade the children to go outside. Instituted a curfew for the adults, too. In those few days, Kyle slept in Ma's room. She sat in a folding chair at the end of the bed, bolt action rifle in her lap, her eyes shifting from the door to the window and back to Kyle.

The curfew was lifted on Saturday and at mass the next day, Father Gleason told the congregation that Lucille's body was found in a cornfield just over the county line. "She's gone home, my brothers and sisters," he said, one hand gripping the pulpit, the other swiping at the tears on his chin.

...

One of the churchgoers coughed, bringing Kyle back to the present. It was an old person's cough, he thought, loud and gurgling. Then his eyes shifted to Father Gleason making his way to the pulpit, wearing the same old vestments, ghostly white and bulky. But they did not touch the floor when he walked, like Kyle remembered. Father had grown a bit of a paunch, his robe tight around the middle now. His hair had thinned and grayed, and the lines in his face were particularly heavy, as if they'd been stitched. But his eyes gleamed.

He began to speak, his voice still brassy, resonant as a foghorn. As the congregation moved through the opening rituals, Kyle followed along, all of the gestures and responses recalled by rote. Like riding a bike.

Before starting the liturgy, Father Gleason did something unexpected. He stepped down from the sanctuary with its white-clothed altar and into the nave. He stood silent for a moment, his fingers woven together in front of him—elbows out, head down. "So we fix our eyes not on what is seen, but on what is unseen." His eyes met Kyle's and a wide smile stretched his plump cheeks. "What is seen is temporary, but what is unseen is eternal."

Kyle felt a bit disappointed. As a child, he'd always convinced himself that Father Gleason's words were meant only for him. It was absurd and smug, he thought now, but recalled how that impression had made each mass feel more special, more sublime.

Ma reached over and placed her hand on his knee, patted it just once, as if she was listening to his thoughts and trying to reassure him. Theirs was a certain brand of love, his and Ma's. They weren't the hugging kind. Kyle knew it had to do with her acting tougher than she was, trying to fill the roles of both mother and father for so long.

...

After communion, Ma continued down the aisle, right past their seats. Though baffled why she would leave the service early, Kyle followed, more than willing to oblige. He opened the big, wood door and they stepped into the noontide. A cool breeze pushed past them and Kyle followed it with his face, feeling the relief that he'd be leaving soon, his visit over. It wasn't the heavy-weight-being-lifted kind, more like an escape or a loophole of sorts, as if he'd found a shortcut around a gridlocked freeway or broken through a bout of writer's block on a script with a deadline.

Either way, he decided this would be his last trip home for a while. No more northern Michigan nights with unbroken starlight. No more wide-open spaces. No blues and greens so deep it hurt to see.

He followed Ma to the parish hall next door and waited while she hurried toward the restroom. "I can't sit through all of mass anymore," she told him.

Ma explained enough so that he understood she was losing control of her bowels. This first mention of Ma's mortality frightened Kyle. For the rest of the day he hovered near her and that night, he watched her fall asleep in her oversized Barcalounger, hunkered down in the beige padding, reclined as far as the chair could go. Her legs were parted, thick wool socks pushed down to the ankles. She had always been a hefty woman and not particularly concerned about make-up and such things. In public, though, she took great pride in looking tidy and dignified.

Kyle felt a tinge of shame, knowing Ma's Sunday best would be scoffed at in his world. He could imagine her smiling with poise, mistaking others' smirks for flattery. This was why he'd never invited her to California, unable to stand the thought of her smoothing her house-dress, clueless she was being mocked by cafe waiters and store clerks.

...

The next morning, Kyle kissed Ma's pleated cheek, promised to call, and left. Neither of them said anything about his next trip home. He'd send flowers, make sure the neighbors checked on her, but it was too much to see Ma like this, the shrinking of life within her.

Kyle boarded a puddle-jumper in Marquette and looked out his window, beyond the tarmac. In the distance, the limestone slabs loomed like guardians over the town. He wondered what Lucille would look like now. Would her hair still be that same platium hue, or might it have shaded some? Would she have moved far away from the Upper

Peninsula? Probably she would have stayed, chosen a quiet life like all the rest. Too soon, she would have gathered the time-honored lines on her face. Maybe her wrinkles would have become more pronounced each time she went to mass and settled into the seat she claimed for herself at Pure Heart of Mary.

He sure hoped so.

The pilot announced through the static of the intercom that all connecting flights into Detroit were delayed. Then a flight attendant approached, her eyes perfectly round, the color of pinecones, and her skin snow-white. Kyle thought her striking and gladly accepted a "complimentary beverage" for the "inconvenience" in his travel plans. He ordered a Bloody Mary with a splash of hot sauce, no garnish. The attendant returned promptly, balancing the drink on a brown, plastic tray. He could see from the clear streaks in the tomato juice that there was too much alcohol. As he brought the glass to his lips, he couldn't help but think of the ornamented chalice that he'd declined at church yesterday—never seemed right, drinking from a cup that so many shared.

The vodka lit up his throat, stole his breath away. But the aftertaste was smooth, taking off the edge already. Kyle took a bigger sip, then let his thoughts of Lucille and all things holy fade when the plane finally lifted off.

~in one fell swoop~

On a sweltering Friday night in July, Ma asked me if I wanted to have a yard sale. She said it would be good experience, witnessing the supply and demand theory first hand. She said we needed the money, too, which I didn't understand. Pa was a foreman at the largest mill in Houghton. All the other foremen's families lived on the bluff in big houses with massive windows and wide, stained decks that wrapped around front, overlooking Lake Superior. We lived in town, an old two-story Victorian with a saggy front porch and a garage that leaned left, too small to park a car in. I remember being at one of those lakeshore houses once, a classmate's birthday party. As I walked by the group of gathered mothers, one said to another, "I heard his father buries money in the yard. What a deadbeat." Later, when Ma picked me up, I told her. She simply replied, "Unfit conversation for a party, don't you think?"

We gathered all the junk that might sell then started debating prices. "Antiquity," Ma quipped, holding up a pair of old ice skates, the kind with straps down the sides, more like a man's belt. "What do you think?" Her smirk was mischievous and I laughed. It felt foreign to do so with such abandon.

"Might have to pay someone to take those," I said. I loved it when Ma acted silly, though it only happened when Pa was gone. The threat of his truck tires crunching against the gravel always loomed, but at least for a little while, she was carefree and playful. However, that night Pa had driven to Green Bay, something about the union and dips in demand for iron ore. All we cared to know is that he wouldn't be back until Sunday.

Ma brought up several boxes from the basement and began digging through one full of ugly sweaters, mostly from Grandma. "On your dad's side," she insisted. Draping a shaggy blue cardigan over her chest, Ma pretended it was the latest fashion craze. She gently brushed her fingers across the dull yellow sunflowers knitted across the mid-section then pinched one of the half-dollar buttons—wood, stained a deep brown—and puckered her lips like a supermodel. She flipped her hair back trying to be salacious but looked more like a liquored up walrus. "A buck fifty," she said in a deep, breathy voice, then wrapped the cardigan around her shoulders with flair, "and this could be yours." We laughed from our bellies. And then a pricing game ensued: .50 cents for dad's old jock strap; a quarter for my bag of army men, pellets of mouse shit in the bottom. We scrawled out "make an offer" on a box of random knickknacks, like some of those souvenir spoons from different states that always tarnish a dark orange and a ceramic salt and pepper shaker set in the likeness of Lot and Lot's wife, the former looking back over her shoulder, of course.

We made $174. Even though I garnered no more than

$10 from selling some old toys and a few fishing lures, Ma
split the money with me. I think about that weekend often.
I still see her flitting between the boxes of junk, letting out
a girlish hee-haw after having played hardball with some
toothless old codger, standing her ground when he tried
dickering her down a nickel for some crocheted pot holders.
When she pressed pencil to paper, tallying our miniscule
proceeds, Ma said, "Integrity is the root of true riches." I
know the words well, as she wrote them in frosting on my
graduation cake in fancy, curlicue letters.

I remember, too, that Sunday, when Pa came home.
Ma and I were boxing up the unsold items when his tires
pressed against the pea stone. After questioning Ma about
our weekend venture, Pa demanded the money. In one fell
swoop, it was gone. Ma's principles were left floating in the
dusty air. I can still hear the thrust of Pa's shovel in the earth,
see the starlight on his naked back as he proved the haughty
ladies on the bluff to be right, planting our money like
rutabaga. My heart still sinks when I recall Ma asking me
for my share of the money back, head down like a scolded
dog. Sometimes, when I think of Ma, the world feels completely
adrift, the sky starless. I wonder how people can just
live their lives—buy groceries, pump their tanks full of gas,
order fancy draft beers—having never known her strength.
And I think, too, how much my heart hurts as it slides up my
throat every damn time I pass a yard sale sign.

~ undelivered ~

Ms. Roe's mailbox is bluish-green—our winters chipped away color—baring spots of metal. It is rusted shut from violent gales, knifing sleet. And inactivity. Yet every Saturday at dawn, the hearty spinster trudges down the hillside and awaits the courier in silence, just outside our matronly circle.

...

In Sheridan County, the mailboxes are clumped together on warped two-by-fours and the posts shift in the earth so that the letter boxes lean like bowed branches. Due to reckless snow-plows, some women paint their boxes splashy colors—our row consists of a grassy green one, pink, a shiny unpainted one, then turquoise (that's Ms. Roe) and black (that's me).

Self-sacrifice has dimmed our eyes, but there's strength in having no voice. The postman steps past her; Ms. Roe stands expressionless 'til he drives away. She curtsies slightly then forges up the ridge, empty-handed once again. And the lines in our foreheads are rigid. You see, the women of the borderland quietly dream their boxes will bring glad tidings or connection, if only by proxy, to the world beyond our margins. So not even a frigid northerly can deter a fron-

tier woman from her weekly trip to the mailbox because
even if she knows it's fruitless, there's hope in the trek.

That day, the bitter wind cut our faces. We were stoic as the postal truck appeared; then the whirling bands of
white closed in behind it. Still, no Ms. Roe.

No one dared watch as the postman tugged at the
lid—the paint flakes sprinkled down, green and blue and
blighted, so sharp atop the snow—and placed the letter inside.

No one dared turn when he closed it again. Like a
floorboard it groaned.

She used a single shot Winchester. Black powder and
blood and patchwork quilts.

And no one dared cry.

The wide-eyed matron ambled over to the blue-green
box and wrenched it open, glanced back for our blessing.
We cast down our eyes. Then, she huffed and tore at the
sullied envelope. We held our breath with sweet expectation but feigned disapproval. "It says, 'Leave the light on,'"
she read aloud. Then, she jerked the paper front to back,
"That's it?" she cawed. We turned our backs as she crinkled
the paper and threw it at our feet. "You wanted me to," she
snarled. The chickadees gargled loud amidst the lull.

"How could we have known?" someone whispered.

...

Our winter-leaden row looks tiny from my window.
I think I'll wrap myself in my sea-colored shawl and curse
the stars, then quickly turn to other things.

$\sim$ mother of a hanged girl $\sim$

Damp winds lashed at town square, tipping hats and rustling papery leaves against the scaffold. Ruth's bonnet lifted and a lock of reddish-yellow hair spilled over her eye. The girl forgot her hands were bound and when she reached to tuck the curl away, rope bit her skin.

"Don't let 'em see you hurting," her mother said.

Ada leveled her shoulders and blew at the loose whorl.

"That's my girl."

Ada knew Ruth was confused. Her only child stood blank-eyed, the shackles heavy as headstones on her wrists. My daughter will die the same way she lived, her simple mind unable to grasp the evil of the world. Perhaps her daftness was a blessing after all.

Ada surveyed the crowd of pinch-faced hypocrites. Brown smoke hung over their heads. The ghostly remnants of dynamite blasts from Beaumont's copper mine layered the air like sediment. She looked from face to face, marking the wrath in the onlookers' eyes. The same good people who sat next to them at church just a few months before, nodding while Ada's husband preached from the pulpit with fire and flair. These same upright folks who said, "Hello, fine ladies," whenever she and Ruth crossed their paths at the postmaster's or the mercantile.

Today, they were judge and jury.

Executioners.

Ada had managed to shield her daughter from the town's fury for months. But ultimately, she had failed. And Ruth would pay with her life. Ada's instinct was to cover her girl's eyes, shield her from the angst and ruthlessness, her muscles aching that she couldn't.

"Heathens!" someone shouted.

"Swindlers! Crooks!" Deacon John cried, raising his fists in the air.

Others cast their eyes to the dirt, unwilling to spur on the rage, yet not brave enough to stop it.

Ada looked just in time to see the deputy slip the noose over her daughter's head, then pull it snug. The fat knot bulged at Ruth's dainty neck like a tumor on a yellow rose.

But Ruth merely looked up at the deputy and smiled. "Ma says I'm going home to be with God." Then she gestured with her head, and said, "Look. The sun's coming out, turning things on. Sorta like a big lamp."

When the coarse hemp rasped against Ruth's jowl, Ada saw her twitch, bow out her chest and stand taller. "Never stole anything," Ruth told the deputy, then looked to her mother for approval.

"No you didn't, baby," Ada called out, working past the swell in her throat.

The deputy yanked a hood over Ruth's head.

"Mama, I can't see!"

...

The Reverend had abandoned his family a year earlier. He took all their money with him, including six-month's worth of St. Michael's tithing. In his wake, he left the church with a leaky roof, a half-renovated belfry, and a penniless wife and daughter. The people of Beaumont could not face the certainty that their man of the cloth, a Lutheran cloth at that, could do such a thing. So they turned a blind eye to the hungry pair—a desperate mother and her defective daughter—and froze them out of the church, for their "selfish ways" and "pushing away the Reverend like they did."

The Williams women lived on the goods they had canned from the summer season and the few meat chickens they kept. Soon enough, they had finished the last of the tomatoes and squash and were down to a puny-breasted egg layer. Ada never learned to hunt or fish, and it wouldn't have mattered anyway, as her husband took the rifle and the poles, too.

Ada convinced herself that they could survive on the food store until the grace of God came to pass: either the Reverend's return or the softening of their neighbors' hearts. But she brought out the last of their provisions from the cellar and placed them on the table—two canisters of beets and a dozen or so potatoes. The sparseness glared at them as sure as the nights turned colder. When she looked at the dwindled reserve, the house closed in on her. The air drew out. She wanted to run for help, scream for mercy. Something to save her daughter and herself. But her feet felt nailed to the floor, her tongue tied. She knew that Ruth was watching her with deep-blue, vacant eyes, wondering what to do, how to act.

That's when instinct took hold, and Ada calmed her breathing, sucking in through her nose and blowing it out through pursed lips. Then, she scooped up several potatoes into her apron, walked to the wash bucket and dropped them in. She nodded at Ruth to do the same. As they rubbed the dirt from each spud and cut the tubers with dull knives, Ada said evenly, "Come tomorrow, we'll beg for money."

For three days, the Williams women trekked to the houses of old friends, Ada leaving her dignity and her daughter outside as she pleaded. But the conversations were always the same, as if the town had come together to rehearse a response. Ada started each exchange by getting right to the point, explaining that she could now see Ruth's ribs when she readied for bed. Then she would add, "It was the Reverend who left. Why is Beaumont forsaking us?"

"You drove him away. Your faith is weak. And the dim-wit's, too."

Ada would bite down on her tongue, the tinny taste of blood flooding her mouth. She'd never get used to the disparaging words to describe her daughter, nor the ease with which they were hurled. "That's not the truth," she'd say. "I held my husband up. It was his faith that wavered, not ours. Not until now."

"You're a liar, Ada! The good Reverend out and said in his last sermon, 'If wives don't lift up their husbands, faith can be shaken.' And God knows. That's why He gave you a fool for a child. May the devil damn you!"

Though she knew folks felt that way, hearing it out loud stunned Ada, stopped her mind from working. But she was finally able to blurt, "But, we're starving. We'll surely die soon if—"

"That's your penance!"

...

On the third day, after every household had turned them out again, Ada and Ruth made their way home. The sun had gone down and the sky was blue-black, the soles of their shoes wearing through, their feet aching and swollen. Ada felt the hollow in her stomach and quick as the winds of an arctic northerly, her grief turned to anger. "Tomorrow, we'll beg in the street," she said. "We'll make our brethren have to see us every day."

So they did. Every afternoon, Ada and Ruth sat in the village's tiny marketplace—legs folded under, hands out—reminding their brothers and sisters in Christ how they were deserting those in need. After days of the townspeople simply walking on by, wordlessly, Ada and Ruth traipsed to the front steps of Saint Michaels, where their husband and father should have been presiding. They sat on the church stairs in their best bonnets and tugged at their petticoats to make them smooth, greeting each arriving family with the kindness of a lover. Only to be slighted. The service started and the parishioners began to sing the opening hymns: the ones Ada knew by heart, the ones about grace and glory and blessed assurance.

"Burn in hell!" Ada roared, pounding on the shut doors. When she heard the muffled sound of Mr. Wilkinson trying to preach—the deacon chosen to serve as the interim minister—Ada pushed her mouth into the crevice where the doors came together and yelled, "Sinners! Praying in the house of the Lord, then turning your backs. That ain't our God in there!"

Below her, Ruth mimicked her mother, putting her lips against the dark slit, shouting out, "I hate you!"

That night, as Ada crept into the Wilkinson's barn, she prayed. Not for forgiveness, but courage. Don't know what God this town's turning to, but Lord, MY Lord, give me strength. Let me feed my baby girl. One of the cows started to grunt, and Ada quickly moved to it, stroked its back lengthwise until it quieted. Her heart beat fast, but she grounded herself, saying over and over again, you have to be here. She tiptoed to an empty stall where two barrels sat side by side then plunged her hands into the first one, a heaping mound of feed. She couldn't help but let the corn kernels slip through her fingers a couple of times before shoveling some into the burlap bag around her waist. Then she stepped to the second barrel, plucking out apples till the bag was nearly full. She felt a rush of emotion: excitement, relief, fear.

But no guilt.

At the edge of her neighbor's property, just past the split-rail fence in front of the house, Ada bent over a hearty rhubarb bush, grabbed several stalks at the base and twisted them with a snap. With each stride toward home, she could feel the heft of the full bag against her thigh. She bit into one of the stalks and puckered at the hard tang, a smile broke across her face.

...

As autumn drew near, the Williams women continued to hunker down in the town square during the day, an empty basket between them and a coal-gray blanket covering their legs and feet. As the passersby shuffled to their destinations, heads high, Ada searched their faces, clearing her throat or calling their names until they looked her way. Ruth smiled up at them like a child.

Though many had complained to Sheriff Thompson, often right in front of Ada and Ruth, telling him to "Rid the town of such rabble," his response was always the same. "They haven't broken any laws."

Come nightfall, Ada sneaked through Beaumont, pilfering her neighbors' barns. With each theft, she grew more confident and daring, swiping loaves of bread from a window set out to cool and from another, a pumpkin pie. Jars of honey from a porch and a salted down ham from an open smokehouse. The Williams women were not overfed, but the hunger pangs had abated some.

Talk began about the pillaged goods. The folks of Beaumont bolted their barn doors against Ada and out by the county line, farmer Richardson set a leg-hold trap in front of his icehouse. Had a cricket not let out a leathery squeak, Ada might not have looked down in time to see the metal snare. Its sharpened teeth would have gnashed her foot. The heyday was over, Ada knew that. And once again, the hopelessness thundered through her head, even louder than before.

One night, as Ada was scampering through a field and back into the village, she told herself to take what she could as time was running out. Don't feel or think, just keep moving. She looked this way, that way, then fixed her eyes on Mr. Turner's house, set back from the road a bit. In front, several big maple trees stood tall and out back, between the slanted outbuilding and the chicken coop, there were several more. Under all that cover, Ada had already robbed the old man's icehouse before—a slab of jerky and some rock mouth bass. But this time, she prowled around the coop like a fox, looking for more traps before unlatching the wired gate. Most of the chickens were in the shelter; some were stirring, ambling across the straw strewn earth. A couple of them clucked at her approach but quieted, bustling out of her path as she slid each foot forward slow and steady, never changing pace. By design, Ada moved more stealthily now.

She glided between the nesting boxes and up to the outside roost then lifted up a fat hen and held it upside down by the feet. Though it spread its wings in protest, Ada held them down and just as coolly backed out of the coop. It only clacked a few times before she was in the yard again, away from the rest, and could wring its neck without an uprising. She gripped its head and pulled down hard then twisted upward, fast and fierce. The body flapped wildly, but she held on tight, and crept backward a few more steps. The blood was dark and gushed in one steady stream, like a pitcher pouring water. She took another step back, thumping against Mr. Turner's round, stiff belly.

"Give it to me, Ada." His voice was husky and low.

Ada's mind whirred. In her fright, she clenched the hen's hocks with all her might, as if she'd fall into a fiery pit should she let go. But Mr. Turner gripped it by its breast with the same ferocity. It was his lifeline, too. They yanked the draining bird back and forth, stretching its cape and thighs like bread dough. Hackle feathers pulled from its body and flitted down around them.

"You're a thief!"

Ada had thought of her actions as survival more than stealing. Being called a crook, outright, was hard to take. But she managed to retort,

"And you're a fraud."

Both shanks pulled loose and Ada tumbled back, but not enough to lose her footing. She kept running.

"God sees you, Ada!" Mr. Turner called after her.

"And you're a hoax!" she yelled back.

...

Ada hadn't slept much in the three nights since Mr. Turner caught her looting his coop. She paced in front of the window for hours at a time, waiting for someone to come, deliver their doom. Then, late that Saturday night she saw the lanterns bouncing down their narrow lane, heard the jittery voices of the two young deputies and shackles jangling against each other. The motion and noise were strange in the prevailing stillness. No one ever visited. By the time they approached, Ada was standing on the porch, gathering her dark tresses into a bun.

"Been expecting you."

"Taking you to the town hall, Ada," the first deputy said. With each word, his pitch rose and fell, his eyes on the chains as he fumbled them from his belt loop.

"Well, get on with it then." Ada finished pushing another hairpin through the black thatch that rested on her nape and held out her hands, wrists up.

"Where's Ruth?" The second deputy's voice was higher, even more agitated.

"My girl's whereabouts don't matter none to you." Ada was matter-of-fact, holding still as she was fettered.

"We've come for her, too."

"But she's done nothing."

"Folks say she's been stealing right along with you."

Instantly, Ada felt weightless. Her face went slack.

"And blaspheming the Lord, I heard," the second deputy added. Then he shook his head and said under his breath, "That girl don't seem like the ransacking kind, though. Let alone, a heathen." He clicked his tongue a couple of times. "Hell, never thought you to be that way neither, Ada."

"Well remember, the Reverend said Lucifer means 'morning star.' And he was God's favorite before he turned into the Devil."

"But Ruth ain't even smart enough to—" The boy didn't finish his sentence. He strode past Ada and pulled the door open but never entered. Instead, Ruth stepped from the archway, her eyes on Ada and her wrists turned skyward, too.

After both women were bound, the four of them began walking to town. Ada felt the anxiety burning her skin from the inside, but she had learned to swallow the nervousness, hold it low in her guts so her mind stayed fresh. She needed to be alert, ready for whatever came their way. She badgered the callow deputies, prodding them for particulars, anything that would help her warn Ruth of the coming onslaught. But the men had already said too much, so they whispered to one another, careful to lag a few steps behind.

With her head kept straight, Ada steered Ruth the best she could. "Ruth, honey, listen. No! Don't look at me." She paused, then started in again. "They're gonna ask you a bunch of questions when we get there. Try to answer with just 'Yes' or 'No.'"

Ruth turned again to see her mother. "They're gonna be mean to us, ain't they?"

"Yes," Ada said. In the scant light of the lanterns behind them, she glanced to see the bewilderment on Ruth's face, and her heart broke open. But Ada had learned to swallow her sadness, too. "Now look away." No time for grieving Ruth's guiltlessness. Or her dull mind. Instead, Ada talked faster, more angrily. She knew Ruth would listen harder if she heard angst in her mother's voice. "If you don't start listening, they'll fine us money we don't have. Or even jail us. Now, when they ask if you been taking things, you say 'No'. Every time, you say, 'No'.

"You're mad at me."

"Damn it, Ruth, don't talk. When they ask if you love God, you say, 'Yes, I do.'

The deputies paused their conversation, and Ada quieted again, to time her dialogue with theirs. But soon enough, Beaumont's town square came into view. The hunter's moon was high, looming over the village like a giant blue eye. Ada slowed her pace, trying to buy more time, but the deputies didn't follow suit.

They approached the town hall, and voices of all different timbres sifted out into the street. The deputies stood on either side of the big doors and pulled them open, both nodding for Ada and Ruth to enter. As they did, the clamor inside halted. The citizens were assembled in tall, rigid chairs, row upon row, and they filled the benches that pushed against the far walls, too. All of them were turned, watching with wild eyes, as though awaiting brides making their way to the altar.

Lanterns lining the center aisle lit every face like the moon outside, each in a different lunar phase. The smell of kerosene was acrid. The deputies veered them to the front of the building and seated them in the two straight-back chairs behind a long table. The first one stared them down like everyone else, insisting with a nod of his head that their arms stay in plain sight, bound or not. The second just stared at the ground.

The room was strangely quiet as Mr. Turner plodded to the podium. He carried the mangled remains of the hen with him, plopped the carcass on the end of the table then wagged his finger at Ada. The putrid stench of the rotting poultry wafted through the open room, overtaking the fuel oil. He turned to the villagers and spoke in the same gruff tone, but more fiery now, talking about the Williams women as if they weren't there.

"These two tried stealing my biggest hen." He pointed at the rumpled mound of feathers. Mr. Turner's pronouncement let loose the crowd's restraint. The townspeople shifted in their seats, grumbled to themselves and to one another. Then Mr. Turner's voice boomed, "And those two been cursing God all over town!"

The room boiled over. Ada spoke to Ruth out of the side of her mouth, loud enough so she could hear over the grousing. "There's gonna be more yelling, Ruth, but never you mind that. Just remember, you didn't take nothing, and you love the Lord."

As she finished the last word, a mealy apple glanced Ada's ear. The sting made her yip, and she lifted her shoulders to guard against any more that may come. She felt herself wincing and twitching as if a gun were pointed at her forehead. Most in the crowd hailed her cowering, yet some looked away. Even in her duress, Ada noticed Ida Lee hastening out the door.

Knowing the bedlam would only grow, Ada stood up. Her face and neck were taut, waiting to be hit by another hurled apple. She clenched all over and shouted out, "I stole from all of you!"

The crowd jeered. But Ada yelled louder. "Had to! And you know why. This ain't about taking chickens or pies, that's all happened before." The horde quieted, some. "We all know this is about the Reverend. He's a deserter. And you can't condemn a man of God. That's fine. Go ahead and blame me." She dipped her head toward Ruth, and said, "But my daughter is innocent. You know that, too! So give us our fine or bring out the pillory if you got to. Lock me in it all day! But let Ruth be!"

Mr. Turner was still at the podium, standing near them both. "Oh, you're sadly mistaken, Miss Ada. This meeting ain't about fines or making amends. This here's about hanging."

Ada's stomach dropped into her feet then fell right through the floor. Cold sweat broke out on her arms and legs. All the words and shouts blurred into a flat buzz, the hum of a solitary wasp. Though she heard Ruth ask, "They mean to hang us, Ma?" she couldn't speak. Then Mr. Murray traipsed to the front of the room, his arm raised above his head, fingers spread, beckoning the Holy Spirit.

"In the name of the Lord," he ministered, "We gotta hang 'em! Rid Beaumont of their sin. And let there be no doubt. These women have trespasses they're carrying, more than just swiping some grub. They've desecrated the Lord! Turned on the good Reverend!"

Mr. Turner gave the rolling snowball a definitive push when he proclaimed, "We do it now, before Sheriff Thompson comes home from Marquette. Not much longer 'fore the sun comes up! Now, I say, in the name of Christ!"

The village heralded the charge. In one fell swoop, Ada and Ruth were lifted up on their backs, bore like litters atop people's shoulders and held up by random hands. Someone gripped Ada's inner thigh, and a couple of thickset fingers lodged in her crotch. She flailed, twisting and turning in their clutches, trying not to fall, but they kept her steady, seizing harder. She arched her body until her head fell backward enough to see Ruth.

"Hold on, baby!" she yelled. Ruth was still, an inflexible plane. In the fists of the mob, the lanterns were bobbing up and down like a mass of frenzied fireflies.

When they reached the grove behind the town hall, they were set atop the scaffold. The deputies held them by their elbows and the backs of their necks as the crowd gathered at the base. The gallows were slanted, tottering with every movement. They hadn't been used for a couple of years, not since the young Ojibwe woman was hanged after her baby girl died. She had brought it on herself, the church council said, hadn't prayed hard enough when the babe was sick.

The deputies bumbled through the execution, desperate to get things right, but even more desperate to distance themselves from the grisly task of hanging a Reverend's wife and daughter.

"Imps!" A wrinkled woman crowed, sparking outbursts from different pockets of onlookers:

"Pagans!"

"Scamps!"

The deputies hulled down the gunny-sacks. The nooses that would crush the women's windpipes swayed like clock bobs. Together, the men began to drag the burlap bags across the platform but sand issued forth, slow and thick, sifting through the wood planks.

"Damnation," the first deputy murmured, "these bags have lost too much sand. Those ropes ain't gonna be stretched enough."

"You cussed fool," the second deputy hissed. He dropped to his knees, madly scooping in the gushing sand. "Brush it up!"

Ada watched the graceless men, her mind still whirring. "Look at me," she called to them. "Look at my face." But she knew they wouldn't. The men scurried at the sand like rodents, turning their heads to glimpse the townspeople, adamant in avoiding Ada's and Ruth's eyes.

There were no options left. Ada knew she could only comfort her daughter now, make it less horrific. She watched Ruth straining against the shackles. As always, her countenance tender and child-like.

The sun broke over the horizon and burned through the fog, casting the deputies' shadows across the scaffold. Ada took comfort when she saw Ruth close her eyes and sniff at the fragrant fall air like a puppy.

"The rope's been stretched good and plenty," the second deputy lied. "These bags have been weighing down the line for years. Can't break, even when you're—" He fell silent. Then the young man twisted up his face like he'd swallowed brine.

"You're sad." Ruth tried to comfort him.

She'd spoken in an even, expressionless tone that sent Ada's heart pounding even harder. She was awed by her daughter's grace and kindness, even now. Her half-wit girl was closer to God than any of these pretenders could ever dream to be. Yet here they are, smearing her goodness like ink on twill.

Dear Lord, hurry. The injustice. It's more than I can bear.

Mr. Turner threw the rotting hen onto the planks, and the young deputy snapped to, then jutted out his chin and spoke firmly. "Like I says, this won't hurt none."

"Hang the shrews!"

"Don't listen to them, Ruth," Ada called to her. "Just focus on my voice!" Ada could tell from Ruth's bunched-up cheeks that she was trying furiously to understand what was happening. As the crowd grew loud, Ada did, too. "Hear me, Ruth! Only me!"

The throng was restless and when the first deputy sucked in a breath then pulled the black hood from his pocket, Ada held steadfast. He turned to Ruth. "Anything you want to say?" he asked, making a downward patting motion for the crowd to hush.

"Never stole anything," Ruth said, then looked to her mother.

"No you didn't, baby." Ada's throat swelled. And the hood was pulled over Ruth's head.

"Mama, it's dark! Where'd the sun go?"

Holding the noose tight at her neck, the second deputy asked Ada if she had any words. And in a single blast, she felt an entire lifetime. The blood drained out of her, down into the timbers, down into the earth below. She was hovering overhead, watching herself and Ruth and the savage swarm. Snippets of cruel scenes played out in her mind's eye. The Reverend in his new life, full of splendor and frills.

She could see him clearly, a crooked and villainous smirk, standing tall and thumbing through a wad of the church's tithing, flicking bill after bill into the open hands of a faceless merchant. By his side, a comely woman stroking the billowy sleeves of a new silk gown, swaying back and forth so her skirt fanned out, the price tag swooshing with it.

The day Ruth was born flashed through Ada's brain, too. When the neighbor acting as midwife guided her babe into the world and slipped in the afterbirth. Ruth's head bouncing just once, yet giving her a lifetime of dull wits and heckling. Then Ada heard the stony words of her pious husband again, when they found out their girl's mind stopped growing—"That child is damned!" he spat, and his voice was breathy and clipped. "Damned, I say!"

Hate burned hot in Ada's chest, crackling and sputtering. Amongst all the rancor, she saw a child in the horde. From where she stood, Ada couldn't be sure, but he looked like the Miller boy. He and his Pa had always sat in the back of the church on Sundays, neither of them ever saying much. The flaming torch in his father's hand cast a shadow across his young face and in the firelight, the whites of his eyes were shiny. He looked bewildered. As if the pitiful lad didn't know what to do. Keep watching? Scorn her like the men and women? Look away? Ada found the strength she needed in the boy's struggle. She thought, He's a talisman, sent by God to bolster me.

Though the hate still boiled, a calm swept over, as if the skillet was lifted off the fire. Ada waited for a lull, then she summoned the town like a prophet:

"Quiet, scalawags! I have a message for all you fine citizens of Beaumont!"

The crowd still roared. Then someone shouted, "Let's hear the devil woman!" and they quieted to a low rumble.

Ada saw the furor in their dimly lit faces, but she was not afraid. Not anymore. She glanced at Ruth, the black cowl atop her pretty head like an ugly scar and her legs trembling, a puddle on the planks between them. Then, she turned back to the crowd, quickly searching for her talisman one last time.

Their eyes locked.

And a wide sneer formed on the boy's round face while his father whispered in his ear. As if Satan himself was the puppeteer, the child drew a tiny hand across his throat, slow and easy.

Ada gasped, then stiffened. "My news is brief!" she shouted. "And it's coming straight from the afterworld." She spoke from outside herself, from some other place, some other time. She could feel her eyes filling up and heard the lack of intonation in her words. "Just as you've taken the light from my Ruth, God will take yours. You will hurt for this. Your children's children will feel the ire. That's a promise." Then a hood was pulled over her head, too. The deputies tightened the loops around both women's necks, and one of them yelled,

"Release!"

$\sim$ a little less blue $\sim$

It was a brisk April night, the week before my 11th birthday, when the flashlight slipped from my hand and tunked across several timbers before I could snatch it up. I sat there at my desk, holding my breath, waiting. Sure enough, Pa barged in, flipped on the light and boomed, "What the hell's going on?" He stepped to me, ripped the journal from my hand. I lunged for it, but he lifted it overhead, scowled until I drew back. I had written a poem about an Italian boy, Giovanni, at my school. He was a virtual punching bag. Not because he was dark complected but rather swarthy with sharp blue eyes. The kids called him a "Siamese mutant" and hissed whenever he was near. He always walked sort of bent, as if readying for someone to pounce on him. And they usually did.

As he recited my work, Pa paced, the wood creaking under his heft. A low, gritty tone: "Soft brown skin, a tender heart—" He stopped, looked at me hard, as if I was a dog that just pissed on the rug. My lungs swelled against my ribcage. "Eyes big and round, a newborn deer." Pa's jowls went taut, his face set like a bull's. He continued treading back and forth. It felt like I was watching from far away, a thousand years gone by. I wondered if this is how Giovanni felt in the hallways, and my heart hurt even more that I could never bring myself to defend him. At least I drew a line by not participating, I always comforted myself.

Pa calmly lay the notebook on my bed, turned to the window. For a moment, he stared at the moon, yellow-white glow flooding the space between us. Then he made his way to the door. I wanted to scream out, to say sorry. But I didn't know why he was mad exactly. Seemed there was more to it than me staying up past bedtime. Didn't matter anyway, he was already gone.

...

A drizzly, gray morning followed. All quiet, except some intermittent bird chatter. I slid into my place at the breakfast table, a straight-backed oak chair, opposite Pa's seat at the head. Per custom, my mother and I waited for him before eating. I dared not even touch my juice. Eventually, he sauntered in, kissed my mother on the forehead and sat with a thud. "Good morning, family." Neither of us replied. From the small glass jar, he scooped out some orange marmalade, smeared it across his made-to-order toast—slightly burnt, no crusts. Only then did Ma and I start to eat, too. The silverware clanked, tinny and awkward.

"Someone's birthday is coming," she said. The unease was greater than usual. Her voice was mild, fragile. "You hoping for a new bow? Or a—"

"Nah." Pa cut in. Then he bit through half the toast, chomping like a mad dog, gummy preserves squeezing out the side of his mouth. "He'd rather have a Barbie playhouse. Right, boy?"

"Charles?" Ma's face twisted like she'd been given an unsolvable riddle.

"Or an Easy Bake oven? How'd that be?"

"Charles!"

I'd never left the table unexcused. But I darted to my room and threw myself on the floor, tears poured down like rain. Through the walls, I heard Pa crackling and Ma begging him to hush. I could only make out the words that his big voice landed on, like "shame" and "rhymes" and "queer." I didn't know what "queer" meant, only that it had to do with writing poems. And that it made me fall out of Pa's favor. After I heard the rumble of his Chevy fading away, I wiped a sleeve across my face, tiptoed back downstairs. Ma was arched over the sink, clenching its sides as if it might escape. I crept out the back door—journal tucked inside my belt—and scrambled to the shed in search of a float, any float would do. My nerves rattled like a baby's toy, not knowing when I'd hear the Chevy's roll again. I scooped up Pa's fishing creel and jaunted through the backyard, down the slope to Mill's Creek. Amid the morning mist, I managed to light a match, then set fire to my poems. I lay the wicker basket into the swell, the spring currents swallowing my voice whole.

After my verses had vanished, all was well again. Pa even asked me to go fishing. "Perch are biting hard," he said. "What d'ya say? Mill's Creek?" He ruffled my hair. From the shed, I heard him shout, "Honey, where's my creel?" There was a strange satisfaction, knowing he was searching for something that just wasn't there.

And I remember how Mr. Bellows called on me, like he did when no one else would talk, asking my thoughts about a line from Emily Dickinson. I'd read her collected works more times than I could count—my teacher knew that, as he'd given it to me. His intentions were good, always trying to challenge our thoughts and beliefs. I desperately wanted to take his bait. Instead, I heard myself say, "Sorry, sir. I don't understand." The lie curdled in my mouth. I kept my eyes cast down, riding out the clumsy silence. When the bell rang, I walked with some guys to Civics class. Giovanni was heading the other way, toward the gym. They started purring at him, making scratching motions with clawed hands. And I joined in. It was a muffled meow at first, but then my chest pulled in every direction. Shame shot up my throat, the sourness stinging my tongue. Then a loud snarl burst free, and I flinched at him. Predator to prey. Though the dusky boy stayed hunched, we still glimpsed one another. His eyes were empty, and as they iced over, a little less blue.

...

Looking back now, I know Giovanni's cloudy eyes were merely reflecting my own.

~ the seventh scar ~

Many a red-hot day did Jay and Dean spend sitting on
the curb by the sewer grate, listening to the foul water running below, dreaming up chancy adventures and most im-
portantly, drumming up ways to pledge their loyalty to one
another. Seems none of the typical boyhood pacts would do.
Spitting and handshakes—not tough enough. A jackknife
to the wrist, bleeding into one another—not original. But
then came the day Dean's dad spoke to them from under
the family's glossy Chevy Camaro, a strange shade of green,
like parakeet feathers and seaweed. His thick, veiny hand
reached out for a wrench, a steady stream of blood flowing
from between his thumb and pointer finger and down his
wrist. He peeked out, gave a hardy chuckle, then pulled
down the sleeve of his flannel to soak up the leaking wound,
saying, "It takes seven scars to be a man, boys."

The gold strike.

Jay and Dean locked eyes. Without words, they knew
what they had to do. The next morning was the last day of
summer and what's more, the dreaded first day of middle
school. They climbed onto Dean's garage roof. Deep down,
Jay knew he was only talking, that he wouldn't actually
jump. But he knew Dean would. When they bickered over
who was going first, Dean held out some, and it made Jay
nervous. So he called him a pussy. He was ready to badger

him more, to talk about courage and honor, things he knew would roil him, but female genitalia did the trick.

They climbed the rickety wood ladder, crabbed to the roof's edge, high-top Converse peeking over, nothing but air. Then an argument erupted over a three count. Did it mean jump on "three" or was there an unspoken "four"? They finally settled on the former. With their innards wobbling like rattletraps, they crouched, ready to leap into manhood. Dean whispered one and two, then shouted "three" and bound off the garage, plummeting fifteen feet to the ground.

Both boys heard his tibia snap—Dean on the ground and Jay still standing on the roof. It was a low, vexing sound that no human part should ever make.

Jay scrambled down the rungs and hovered close by. Dean's shinbone was poking through the skin like a polished shark's tooth from an airport gift shop. The blood didn't spill out right away, so both of them stared at the white wedge, looking at each other with big eyes, waiting for something more. When the dam finally broke, it came in spurts, like someone stomping on a bunch of ketchup packets. After the sting kicked in, Dean bleated, high and shrill, begging Jay to push it back in.

For a moment, Jay stood motionless, watching his friend writhe like a baited grub. Then he snapped to, turned on his heel and ran for help. As he made his way through the yard, heading for the front of Dean's house, the pity and fear drained from him like a tire leak, slow and easy. There was some disgrace for having bailed on his could-have-been blood brother, but "Thank God it wasn't me" thrummed loudest in his brain, staving off any space for shame.

Between short puffs and weighty heaves, he managed to tell Dean's dad what had happened, the man's face thinning and paling with each hurled word. When he jolted up from the table and dashed out the door, Jay fell in behind. And then, something loosened in his guts. He felt it swivel and twist like a hungry side-wider until it landed someplace else—someplace darker and less steady. He couldn't define it. Nor could his mind measure it. Even at twelve years old, though, his sensibility could grasp the start of a downslide. It felt bad. And it felt for keeps. He wanted to rail against it, but he didn't know how to battle something that he couldn't even see.

...

Though the Fosters were re-stationed the following year, Dean never really left Jay. Every time his moral compass teetered, there was Dean—his face, his scream, his shinbone. Like when Jay cheated on the AP Calc. exam, plugged all that sine, cosine crap into his fancy new calculator. Mrs. Good never suspected a thing, but Dean flashed through his head, wispy black hair standing on end as he tumbled from the roof like a rock. Or all the times he pushed past the hunched over folks at the casino, elbowing his way into the jackpot drawings, pretending he was helping them up the stairs. And the time he turned back the odometer, selling some starving graduate student his piece of shit Pacer. Poof! Dean appeared, making tsk sounds with his tongue, wagging a disapproving finger on one hand, and the other still holding his lower leg as it bleeds out, darkening the dirt beneath.

And the insider trading.

And the Ponzi schemes.

And all of the "But it's you I love" speeches to vulnerable, bewildered lovers...

Yet the tinderbox moment came the night he betrayed his fiancé, weakness and truth colliding like a supernova, leaving nothing but a big, black, sucking hole. It was his own bachelor party when he fucked the waitress from Bob's Tavern, the one with the crooked bangs and paper thin camisole, a faded crucifix tattoo peeking out of her thick cleavage. He didn't know her name, only that she had battered knees and egg breath. And that her baby cried in its crib nearby.

Too drunk to shower off the Aqua Net and imitation Jean Naté from the local Revco, he stumbled into bed next to his betrothed, pants at his ankles, breath of a dragon. In the morning, the note on the refrigerator read—*May you find what you're looking for*—and the engagement ring was on the table. So he hocked it, bought some amateur porn from Hollywood Video then drank himself into blankness at the Rusty Cog. All the while, he fought the sour memory of his father's luggage on the sidewalk, truck running, and mom standing in the window, a crumpled white shirt in her grip, lipstick other than her own smeared across the collar like blood on snow.

With his fingers tingling and his face sagging loose, Jay focused hard on staying in his lane on the trek home. But when he finally turned onto his street, that last drink, the damnable vodka Gimlet—light on the simple syrup, lime wedge the size of a tire—soaked up his brain, flipped his judgment like a switch, from a bit dim to an all-out soupy fog. His house came into view, all perception and distance blurred. He sped directly at it, crossing end-long over the neighbor's lawn then into their driveway.

A slight bump. A low whimper. He'd crushed the hind legs of their Labrador, Max. They dragged behind the dog like kite strings as it tried inching toward the house with only front paws. Panic sliced through the alcohol like a machete. Everything was fast and frantic, yet the air turned thick, like oil seeping through his lungs. His soul told him to reach for the rags in the backseat, but instead, he grabbed the tire iron. Dean's face flickered wildly in his mind's eye as he reared the steely tool high overhead. He glanced at the house. No sign of movement, only the white, blue glow of the television splashing against the living room wall. His heart thrashed against his ribcage, pounded in his mouth, his ears. Then he turned back to the broken hound, dug his upper teeth into his lower lip, clenching his body for the kill—

A boxy SUV appeared at the entrance of the cul-de-sac. For an instant, the yellow light flooded the scene like water. And just as quickly, the vehicle turned left, disappearing behind a row of manicured Hydrangea bushes, then went dark. In that blink of time, Jay saw himself, illuminated, like the star of some brutal slasher flick. He was motionless, arm still raised. He glanced down at the broken animal as it let out a thin mewl—eyes wide, searching, sleek as crow feathers.

"For the love of God," Jay whispered through clutched lips. "Who am I?" His chest went hollow, his legs weightless. Nerves pricked and bubbled like soda, and he let out the air he'd been holding. Slowly, the tire iron came down, his mouth dry as sand, tongue dipped in glue. He scooped Max into his arms and stumbled to the porch as if unconscious, carrying him like an offering, the trampled legs bent and drooping. He set the dog down gently and before turning away, stroked its back, the fur soft against his fat-knuckled hand. In a split second, all his filth boiled up, lodged in his throat, his neck, his arteries. Max lifted his head. And Jay was cornered, the dregs of his misdeeds like a shrinking cage. He held back the tears as he spoke—voice cracking, words teetering—"Sorry, ol' boy."

...

The sky is dark gray, the color of oyster meat. And the rain is light but constant, the grass wet and glistening. Dean's house is abandoned now. There's a "For Sale" sign in front—Beaumont Realty—hanging by a hinge, the post leaning like a top-heavy drunkard. Spindly ragweed has overtaken the yard and porch. Jay traipses to the garage, just as threatening as four decades earlier. His pulse doubles down, pumping hard in his face. The same wooden ladder they used as kids is still hanging on the side wall. He stands it upright, shimmies the side-rails into the dirt then starts to climb, slow but deliberate, gripping each rung tight. He's more winded with each heft, partly because he's forty-eight and twenty-plus pounds overweight, but mostly from fear of the restitution at hand. He creeps toward the edge, looks out over his youth. Across the way is his childhood home, the wood slats sided with vinyl now, shamrock green, and there's a set of saw-horses in the yard, plywood resting across them and what looks to have been a push mower, its guts strewn about like a field-dressed deer. A wave of nostalgia swells up but he snuffs it out, pulls off his shoes and tosses them aside. It feels right being barefoot. He takes another step. The shingles are slick but still they bite at the soft pads of his feet. He curls his toes over the eavestrough, stares down at the dampened twigs, leaves and black moss that have gathered through the seasons.

Sucking in hard, he pulls back his arms like slingshots taking aim, then bows at the waist, readying to fling himself into absolution. He counts to two in his head, hears Dean's voice shout "three" then starts to swing forward. His chest is out over the edge yet hesitation anchors his lower half.

And he slips. His backside strikes the rigid surface with a low thud. He glances off, the trajectory in motion. Firing out his hand, Jay clutches the eavestrough. It crumples a foot or two before catching. The crunch of metal sounds out. Then he dangles, mid-air, caught between pulling himself up—or letting go—

~ acknowledgments ~

"teeth" • *Sky Island Journal*, 2020

"check mate" • anthologized in *On Loss*, an anthology, 2019

"unfolded" • winner in *Exposition Review*'s "Flash 405" contest, 2016

"tiny mirrors" • *The Darling Axe*, 2019

"featherweight" • winner in *Pulp Fiction*'s "The Hummingbird" flash fiction contest, 2019

"from under a porch" • *Sky Island Journal*, 2019 (Best of the Net, Pushcart Nominee)

"homecoming, and going" • *Faith, Hope & Fiction*, 2018

"in one fell swoop" • *From Whispers to Roars*, 2019

"undelivered" • *Café Aphra*, 2014

"mother of a hanged girl" • winner in Arch Street Press's "First Chapter" contest, 2018

"a little less blue" • *Sky Island Journal*, 2021

"the seventh scar" • anthologized in *Scribes Valley, Story Harvest: Fresh-Picked Tales*, 2021

~ colophon ~

Interior text is set in the Linden Hill Family. The cover font is Garamond.

~ About Etchings Press ~

Etchings Press is a student-run publisher at the University of Indianapolis that runs a post-publication award—the Whirling Prize—as well as an annual publication contest for one poetry chapbook, one prose chapbook, and one novella. On occasion, Etchings Press publishes new chapbooks from previous winners. For more information about these contests and the Whirling Prize post-publication award, please visit etchings.uindy.edu.

Previous winners and publications:

Poetry

2022: *A Place That Knows You* by Tiwaladeoluwa Adekunle

2022: *The Vaudeville Horse* by Elizabeth Kerlikowske

2021: *My Mother's Ghost Scrubs the Floor at 2 a.m.* by Robert Okaji

2020: *Vaginas Need Air* by Tori Grant Welhouse

2019: *As Lovers Always Do* by Marne Wilson

2018: *In the Herald of Improbable Misfortunes* by Robert Campbell

2017: *Uncle Harold's Maxwell House Haggadah* by Danny Caine

2016: *Some Animals* by Kelli Allen

2015: *Velocity of Slugs* by Joey Connelly

2014: *Action at a Distance* by Christopher Petruccelli

Prose

2022: *Triple Point* by Laura Story Johnson (essays)

2021: *Bad Man Love Stories* by Curtis VanDonkelaar (fiction)

2020: *Three in the Morning and You Don't Smoke Anymore*
   by Peter J. Stavros (fiction)
2019: *Dissenting Opinion from the Committee for the Beatitudes*
   by Marc J. Sheehan (fiction)
2018: *The Forsaken* by Chad V. Broughman (fiction)
2017: *Unravelings* by Sarah Cheshire (memoir)
2016: *Pathetic* by Shannon McLeod (essays)
2015: *Ologies* by Chelsea Biondolillo (essays)
2014: *Static: Stories* by Frederick Pelzer (fiction)

Novella
2022: *Goodbye to the Ocean* by Susan L. Lin
2021: *Miss Alma May Learns to Fight* by Stuart Rose
2020: *Under Black Leaves* by Doug Ramspeck
2019: *Savonne, Not Vonny* by Robin Lee Lovelace
2018: *Edge of the Known Bus Line* by James R. Gapinski
2017: *The Denialist's Almanac of American Plague and Pestilence*
   by Christopher Mohar
2016: *Followers* by Adam Fleming Petty

Chapbooks from Previous Winners
2022: *slighted.* by Chad V. Broughman (fiction)
2020: *Fruit Rot* by James R. Gapinski (fiction)
2016: *#LOVESONG* by Chelsea Biondolillo (microessays with
photos and found text)

Chad V. Broughman was the recipient of the Rusty Scythe Prize Book award in 2016 and in 2017 was awarded the Adobe Cottage Writers Retreat honor in New Mexico. As well, Chad was previously selected by Etchings Press for his chapbook, *the forsaken*. His fiction can be found in journals nationwide—such as *Carrier Pigeon, East Coast Literary Review, River Poets Journal, Burningword,* and *From Whispers to Roars*—and he is anthologized in the *Write Michigan Short Story Anthology* and *On Loss* as well as in *Scribes Valley Anthology,* 2021. He holds an MFA from Spalding University and served as a co-editor for the poetry/prose blog *Café Aphra* based out of the United Kingdom. Chad teaches English and Creative Writing at the secondary and post-secondary levels and when he is not writing or spreading the joys of language, he is spending time with his groovy wife and two rambunctious young sons.